To my daughter, Mari (and Granny Marie).

We have much to do.

Philomel Books
An imprint of Penguin Random House LLC, New York

First published in Great Britain by HarperCollins Children's Books in 2020.
First published in the United States of America by Philomel Books, an imprint of
Penguin Random House LLC, 2020.

Text and illustrations copyright © 2020 by Oliver Jeffers.
Design by Rory Jeffers.
Page 8 pencil lettering based on a quote from
Richelieu; Or, The Conspiracy by Edward Bulwer-Lytton, 1839.

Visit us online at penguinrandomhouse.com

Manufactured in China

ISBN 9780593206751

1 3 5 7 9 10 8 6 4 2

You are only free to dream and plan (for the future)
when you are not battling to survive (the present).
To all those fathers and daughters on this orb whose odds are
stacked less fortuitously than ours, our aim is to even the field.
Love, Oliver and Mari

In remembrance of Óscar and Valeria,
who tried and never made it across

WHAT WE'LL BUILD

PLANS FOR OUR TOGETHER FUTURE

OLIVER JEFFERS

PHILOMEL

What shall we build, you

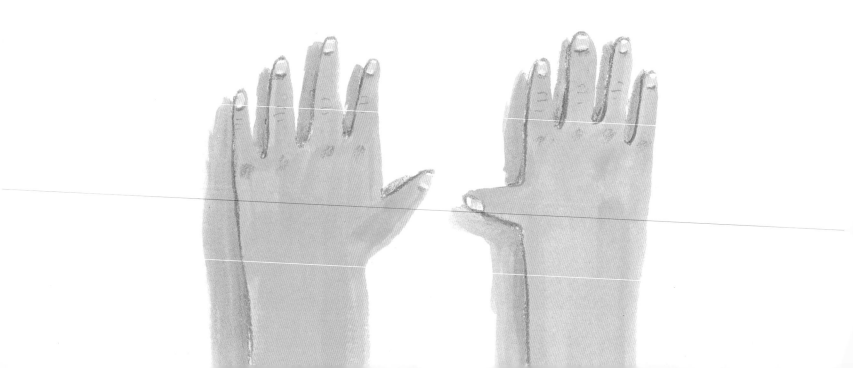

and I?

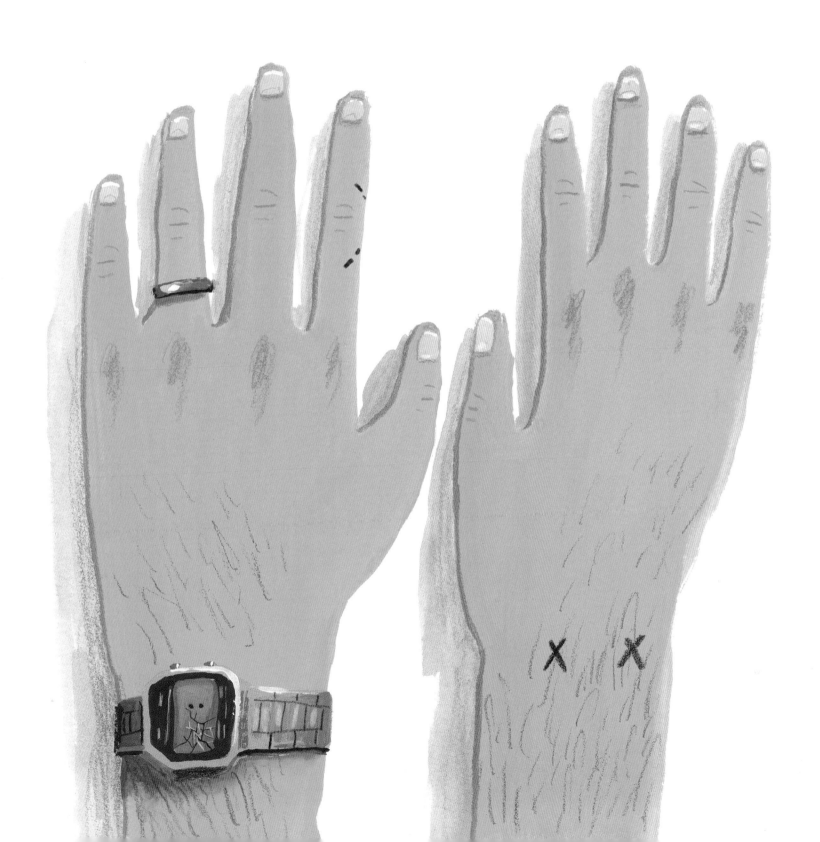

Let's gather all our tools for a start.

For putting together

and taking apart.

Let's build a door

where there was none.

We'll build a house

to be our home.

I'll build your future and you'll build mine.

We'll build a watch to keep our time.

We'll build some love to set aside,

and build a hole where we can hide.

A fortress to keep
our enemies out,

and higher walls for when they shout.

But you don't always lose,
and you don't always win.

So we'll build a gate to let them in.

We'll build a table to drink our tea,
and say . . .

We'll build a tower
to watch the sky,

and other worlds
that pass us by.

Let's build a tunnel to anywhere.

Let's build a road up to the moon.

Let's build a comfy place to rest,
for we'll be tired soon.

Let's build a boat that can't be broken,

that will not sink or be cracked open.

A place to stay when all is lost,

to keep the things we love the most.

We'll put these favorite things beside

the earlier love we set aside.

I think that we may want them later,

when times are hard and needs are greater.

But, first things first, let's build a fire,

for we've planned a lot and now we're tired.

It'll keep us warm like when we're born,

then we'll say good night, as all's all right.

These are the things
we'll build,

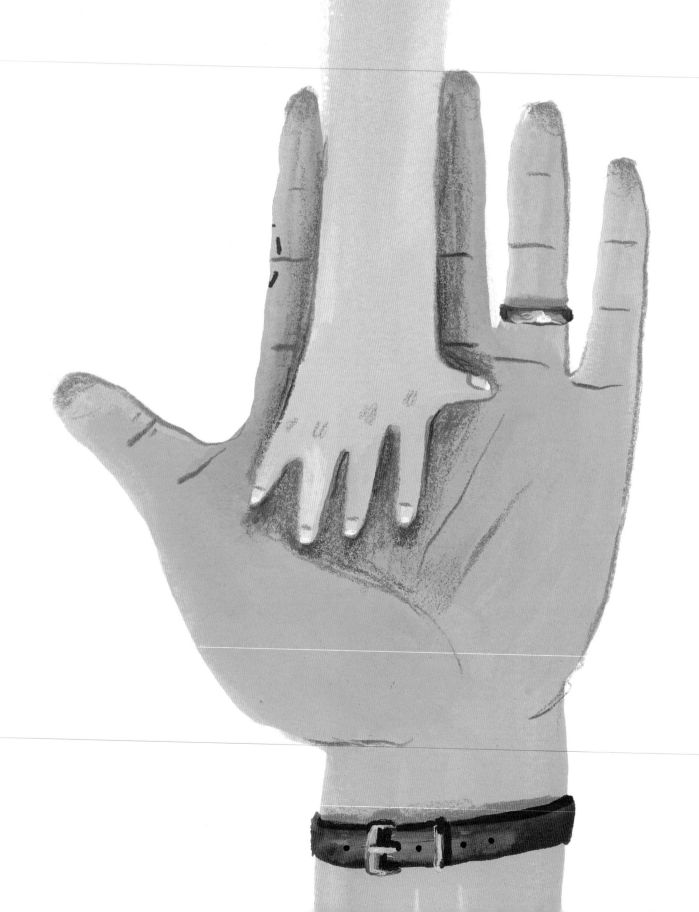

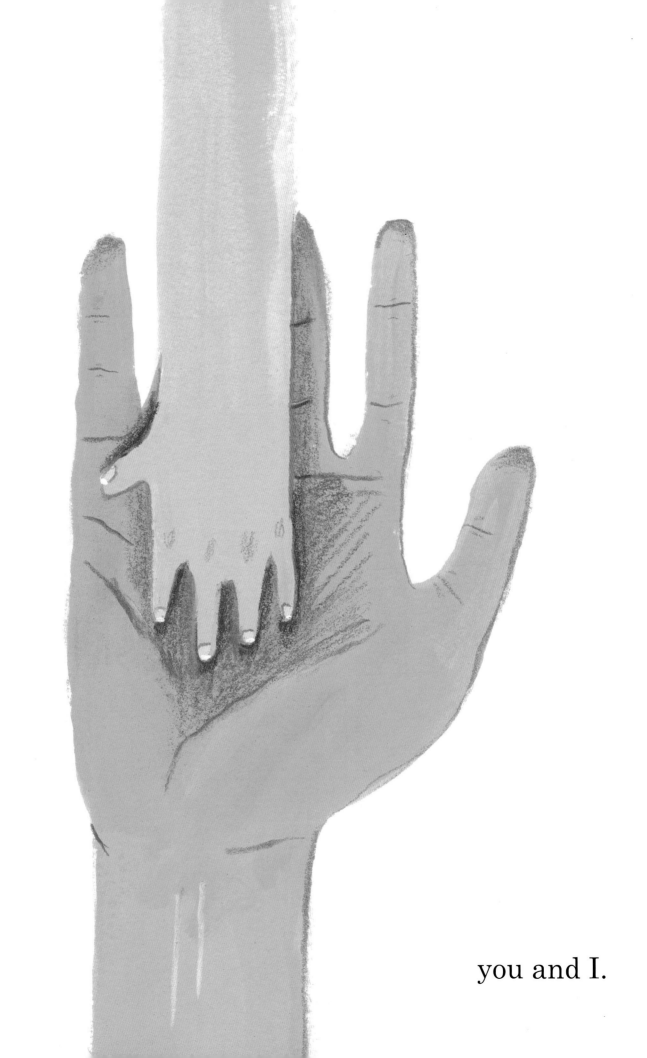

you and I.